MIRACULOUS!

Catholic Mysteries for Kids

Kathryn Griffin Swegart OFS

To Liam and Declan

Table of Contents

INTRODUCTION

Miraculous! Catholic Mysteries for Kids

In the western part of Maine, a river flows through evergreen forests, over boulders and down to the Atlantic Ocean. On a sunny day, it sparkles like diamonds. The Swift River looks like any other stream, but don't be fooled. Prospectors, both young and old, have discovered large nuggets of gold in the bedrock.

A different type of treasure can be found between the covers of this book. You are about to read ten stories that are gold nuggets in Church history, stories of miraculous escapes, of heavenly visits, of a flying priest and much more. Many have been studied by experts who can only conclude that no scientific explanation is possible.

All these miracles are gifts from God, freely given to strengthen our faith and to encourage us on this journey to our true home, to the heavenly kingdom.

THE HOUSE OF THE
BLESSED VIRGIN
Italy - 1294

All was quiet on the sloping pasture near the Adriatic Sea, in the territory of Recanati, Italy. It was December 10, 1294. A shepherd named Angelo looked up at the night sky and yawned. His two companions slept peacefully while he kept watch over the flock of sheep. Angelo shivered and pulled his cloak tightly to his body. Night watch was lonely and dull, a time when nothing ever happened. He gazed at the sky, sprinkled with stars.

3

Suddenly, a glowing object appeared high above the water. At first, Angelo thought it might be a shooting star, but it moved more slowly, drawing closer to the shore. In fact, it was headed directly at him! The glowing object glided down and disappeared into nearby woods. Angelo stared in disbelief. He jumped up and awakened his two companions.

"A star has fallen from the sky and landed in the woods!" he cried.

Pietro was the oldest of the three shepherds and the most sensible. "Angelo, I have told you never to awaken me unless we are in mortal danger. I hear no howling of wolves," Pietro said. "Let me go back to sleep."

"Something strange has happened. Trust me."

Marcus, youngest of the three, was always ready for adventure. "I want to see. Let's go!"

Marcus and Angelo took off into the woods. Pietro reluctantly followed. The young shepherds ran through the forest until they came to a clearing. A little chapel rested on the surface of a grassy glade. It had no foundation and had a small steeple from which hung two bells. It was made of red stone and had one window. The roof was painted blue.

Pietro took off his hat and scratched his head. "What is this?"

"A chapel," Marcus said.

"I know that, but where did it come from? I tramped through these woods my whole life and never saw it before," Pietro said.

"I believe it is a miracle," Angelo said. "Some force has carried it over the sea to these woods—to this hiding place."

"Why would anyone want to hide a church?" Marcus asked. "And who would be strong enough to carry it through the sky?"

"Perhaps it was in danger...and maybe angels carried it," Angelo said.

They looked at each other, not knowing what to think. What would *you* do if a mysterious house dropped in your backyard? You would open the door and go inside, of course. That is exactly what the three shepherds did.

Angelo opened the door and entered. Small wooden cupboards lined the walls. On the south wall was a stone altar, above it hung a wooden cross with a painted image of Jesus. Below the cross was a small painting of the sorrowful mother and Saint John the Evangelist.

None of the shepherds said a word to each other. Instead, they fell on their knees and began to pray, not just for a few minutes, but all night. Time seemed to come to a halt, but God can be predictable in His ways. The sun did come up and shook the shepherds from their spells.

Under the morning glow of sunrise, they ran four miles to the place where their boss lived. His name was Martin. He was a stern man but did not have a mean bone in his body. That morning, he sat eating a pear when the shepherds burst into his house filled with news. Martin listened politely but shook his head. "Someone must have built the house, and we did not notice," he said.

"No, sir! It is a very old house and it has no foundation. Angels moved it. That is the only answer," Angelo replied.

Martin took a bite of his pear and chewed slowly, pondering the situation. If he argued with them, that would waste time. If he investigated, he could lay the crazy story to rest and go on with business.

"Okay, show me the way," he said.

Upon arrival at the chapel, Martin could not believe his eyes. Indeed, it was an ancient house, perhaps a thousand years old.

5

He inspected the outside, observed no foundation, yet it did not tumble to the ground. Martin sensed something supernatural was afoot. *Maybe angels did move it,* he thought. Cautiously, they entered. Martin felt the presence of God and fell to his knees in prayer.

With haste, they hurried home to tell their story to the people of Recanati. All who heard ran through the forests with cries of joy. Those from the village came to believe, and their belief was rewarded with miraculous cures. No one knew what the chapel was or where it came from, but that did not matter. In a short time, pilgrims traveled far and wide to pray at this holy site.

Again, this tale takes a strange twist. The holy House had come to rest in a solitary spot in a thickly wooded forest—a perfect place for robbers to hide. As pilgrims approached, thieves ambushed them, stealing money, clothes and even killing them. Pilgrims feared for their lives and stopped coming. Once again, angels took action.

In August 1295, the sacred House was moved to a little hill about one mile away, a spot owned by two brothers. Imagine the thrill of these two brothers—we will call them Giuseppe and Francisco—when they awoke to view the little House sitting in their pasture. Their hearts were flooded with gratitude. News spread of the strange event. Pilgrims came by the hundreds, many carrying gold and silver.

Giuseppe had an idea. "Let's take these treasures for ourselves. No one will notice."

Francisco agreed. "What good is money to a house? Maybe that's why the angels brought it here. They knew we needed the money."

It seemed like they would get away with this scheme, but someone upstairs noticed. You can probably guess what happened next. Angels moved it to the next hill, two miles from the sea, in Loreto, where it stands to this very day.

By now you may be wondering about the origins of this chapel. It is called the Holy House of the Virgin Mary and it came from Nazareth in faraway Israel. In this humble dwelling, Mary was born. It is the place of the Immaculate Conception and the Annunciation. Here the Holy Family lived the hidden life for thirty years.

Why did angels move the house from Nazareth to Italy?

For centuries, Saracen warriors attacked the Holy Land, destroying Christian churches, including a large church built over Mary's House. For centuries, the holy House was preserved from harm, but God knew it was a matter of time before this most sacred House would be destroyed. He sent His angels to protect it, just as He sends our guardian angels to protect us.

OUR LADY OF GUADALUPE
MEXICO - 1531

A cold north wind whipped in the face of a peasant farmer as he trudged to Mass on the morning of December 9, 1531. It was an ordinary day like every other day. Sorrow still clutched his heart as he thought of his wife who had recently died. Now he lived with his elderly uncle on a small farm near Mexico City. The peasant was Juan Diego and he was hungry. That is not surprising for his garden soil was filled with rocks. Many days he could barely find food to eat. Juan pulled the cloak close to his body to keep out the frigid air. It was not a cape made of wool or cotton. In fact, it was made of cactus fibers. People of Mexico called it a tilma. As Juan shuffled along, he felt discouraged. Every day the walk to Mass seemed longer.

"I am getting old," he sighed.

At that moment, a strange thing happened. The songs of spring birds wafted down from Tepeyac Hill not far from the road.

"Songbirds in the winter? Impossible!" Juan said out loud.

He hesitated, wondering whether to investigate. He did not want to be late for Mass. Curiosity got the better of him and he climbed Tepeyac Hill. At the top, he glanced up, expecting to see grass covered with frost and a few trees. That was not the case. A woman stood before him, but not just any woman. She was more radiant than a glorious sunrise.

The Lady spoke to him, "I am the Virgin Mary, mother of the very true deity."

Juan did not know what to do or say. In fact, he thought this vision might be a mistake. After all, he was only a humble peasant.

She continued, "Go to the bishop and tell him I want a chapel built on this hill in my honor."

Now Juan felt really nervous. He had never spoken to a bishop in his life. As a mother encourages her child, Mary smiled and gestured toward the road. Juan kept walking toward the bishop's house. All the way he kept thinking there must be some mistake. Why would a heavenly visitor choose him as a messenger? Juan arrived at his destination and knocked on the door, hoping no one heard. Much to his dismay, a housekeeper opened the door and scowled.

"Who are you?" she asked.

"I am Juan Diego. I am here to speak with the bishop."

She narrowed her eyes. "Sit in that chair. I will tell him."

Juan sat for what seemed like an eternity. Finally, Bishop Juan de Zumárraga opened the door.

"Come in, but I don't have much time. I am a busy man, you know."

"My name is Juan Diego…"

"I know, good man, now please get to the point. How can I help you?"

"I have a message from the Blessed Virgin Mary."

"From whom?"

"…the Blessed Virgin Mary."

Bishop Juan prayed for patience. It was going to be a long day. He had so many meetings to attend and churches to visit. Now this?

"Tell me your story," he said.

Words tumbled out of Juan Diego's mouth. He spoke of mysterious birds, the luminous Lady and her request.

"She wants me to build a church? That costs money, you know," the bishop said.

Juan Diego said nothing.

"I do not believe you had a vision," said the bishop. "Perhaps it was a dream. I will see you to the door."

Now outside the rectory, Juan breathed a sigh of relief. At least the meeting was over, but what was he to tell the Blessed Virgin? As he suspected, the Lady had chosen the wrong person. Perhaps she could appear to someone more important in the village. He walked briskly to Tepeyac Hill. You probably have guessed who was waiting for him.

Juan fell to his knees. Despite the bright glow that lit up trees and grass and even his face, Juan was not afraid. After all, he was talking to his loving mother.

"Dear mother, the bishop did not believe me. Perhaps if you chose a more important person, he would listen."

"No, Juan, my Son has chosen you. Go back to the bishop and ask again."

That he did, but every step of the way, doubts filled his mind. All he could do was trust God…despite the certainty of failure.

Once again, Juan waited many hours to see the bishop. Once again, he spoke nervously to the bishop, repeating Mary's request. Juan waited to be abruptly dismissed, but that did not happen. Instead, the bishop had a request of his own.

"Go back to the Lady and ask for a sign to prove that she is real."

Juan Diego bowed reverently and walked home, not to Tepeyac Hill. You see, he was tired from all this excitement. He would visit the Blessed Virgin tomorrow. Upon arrival at his humble cottage, Juan discovered his uncle was seriously ill with a high fever, a fever that could lead to death. For two days, Juan stayed by his uncle. Juan realized that his uncle was near death and needed a priest.

As Juan set out to summon a priest, he decided to avoid the road near Tepeyac Hill. He planned to meet the Blessed Mother after he found help for his dying uncle. Have you ever noticed that mothers know how to read the thoughts of their children? Mary knew exactly what was happening and suddenly appeared in front of Juan.

"Am I not here? I am your mother. Go back to Tepeyac Hill where you will find flowers. Gather them in your tilma. Keep them hidden until you show the bishop. Do not worry about your uncle. He is in my care."

Juan now felt like a new man. He was a man bathed in the love of Jesus and His mother. Quickly, he set off to climb Tepeyac Hill, where he witnessed another miracle. Yesterday, the hill was covered with brown grass and weeds. Now brilliant red roses blossomed, flowers that did not grow in Mexico. He gathered them in his tilma and went to the bishop's house. Juan Diego had grown accustomed to the skeptical looks of the bishop's housekeeper. Juan waited patiently. Finally, the door opened.

This time, Juan did not sit down. Instead, he stood before the bishop and opened his tilma. Roses cascaded out of his cape. Bishop Juan stood enthralled by the sight and looked at the poor peasant. Lo and behold, he witnessed another miracle! Emblazoned on Juan Diego's tilma was an image like nothing he had ever seen before. It was the image of Our Lady dressed in a rose-colored robe; her hands were clasped in prayer. Stars were strewn across her blue mantle. Bishop Juan fell to his knees.

As you can well imagine, the bishop came to believe in the apparition. At first a small church was built on Tepeyac Hill. Later, a basilica was built on the site. In 1976, a new basilica was completed. Over the centuries, millions of pilgrims have come to view Juan Diego's tilma. It is the most visited pilgrimage site in the world.

THE ANGELIC DOG
ITALY - 1852

Darkness fell over the city of Turin, Italy, in the year 1852. Turin was a dangerous place to live. Robbers lurked in the alleys and rats foraged for food in the gutters. Few dared walk the streets at night, especially without a companion. One man walked alone through the streets. His name was Father John Bosco, a priest strong in build and kind of heart, a man dedicated to helping homeless boys learn about God's mercy, work that meant long days and nights. Many affectionately called him Don (Father) Bosco.

Sad to say, he also was hated by those who despised the Catholic Church. The priest knew of this hatred, but never stopped his works of charity. Don Bosco kept his head down and kept walking, listening for hints of an ambush.

From out of the fog, a figure moved toward him. A gray dog trotted out of the mist, appearing out of thin air—or so it seemed. The priest stopped and stared. A huge, ugly dog with a long snout and pointed ears blocked the way. Don Bosco thought for sure it was a wolf prowling Turin in search of food. The priest looked for a place to escape, but it was too late. The beast stood in front of him but did not growl. In fact, he wagged his tail. Don Bosco gathered up his courage and spoke.

"Hello, my friend. I do not know where you came from, but I could use some company. I will call you Grigio—Gray One—because your fur is gray, like the sky after sunset."

Together, man and beast walked safely through the streets of Turin. Upon their arrival at Don Bosco's home, Grigio disappeared into the mist. He did not look for food or shelter. That was a curious thing. Think about your dog or your neighbor's dog. Most dogs like to eat treats and sleep on a soft doggie bed. Not Grigio. Puzzled by Grigio's behavior, a question popped into Don Bosco's mind. Was it a real dog...or a heavenly visitor here to protect him? Would he ever see Grigio again? The good priest would soon get his answer.

On many evenings, Don Bosco had to walk the streets of Turin alone, never knowing if he would make it home alive. Time after time, Grigio appeared by his side, alert for any danger, always appearing out of nowhere.

One night, two men hid in the shadows, waiting to attack. Once again, it was a murky night. Rain beat down on Don Bosco. Suddenly he realized he was being followed. Somebody was walking behind him. In fact, two men stalked him, keeping pace, getting closer. Suddenly, they pounced on him. One man threw a cloak over the priest's head and the other tried to gag him.

Out of the black night came a howl. It was the unmistakable call of Don Bosco's guardian dog. Grigio sprang on one man, snarling and snapping until the man let go of the cloak and lay on the ground trembling in fear. The dog latched onto the second man and sank sharp teeth into his flesh, causing the man to collapse and beg for mercy.

"Call off your dog!" he shouted.

"I will call him off if you allow me to go my way in peace."

Grigio curled his lips and breathed into the man's face.

"Yes, yes, but call him off."

Don Bosco clapped his hands. "Come, Grigio."

Grigio growled once more and went to his master's side. Together they walked home in safety.

Over the course of many years, Don Bosco was the object of ambushes by men with guns and knives. Grigio always appeared in the nick of time. On one memorable night, a man ran after him carrying a club. The priest ran down a hill only to find more men waiting for him. Now he was surrounded by thugs carrying sticks. Just then a howl split the night air. Grigio jumped into the center next to the priest. The animal paced round and round, flashing his razor-sharp teeth at the attackers. Once again, they fled in fear.

As stories spread of these incidents, Grigio became famous in the city of Turin. Don Bosco's boys often played with him and wished that he could live with them. That never happened. After every appearance, Grigio vanished. One day Grigio disappeared into the woods. Month after month passed. It seemed that he was gone forever. Year after year, not a soul saw this heroic dog that saved the life of their beloved priest. Ten years passed without a trace of Grigio, but Don Bosco never forgot his loyal friend.

One night, the priest walked the streets of Turin to visit friends who lived in a farmhouse far from the city. No moon shone to light the way. Fear crept into his heart. He imagined attackers behind every tree.

"Oh, how I wish Grigio was here."

It is said that God hears even the smallest prayer whispered in our minds. And so it happened that Grigio materialized on the road, wagging his tail with glee. Father John hugged the dog, thanking God for this wondrous friend.

They arrived safely at the farmhouse. Grigio trotted into the house and curled up next to a crackling fire. The farmer and his family were overjoyed to see them both. It was a delicious feast spread out on a red-checkered tablecloth, complete with plates of spaghetti, bread and salad. After serving Don Bosco, the farmer had an idea.

"I will give Grigio some meatballs. He will surely enjoy that!"

He put a bowl of food on the floor and whistled for Grigio. To his immense surprise, the dog was gone, never to be seen again.

THE MYSTERIOUS STAIRCASE
SANTA FE - 1878

One day in the year 1878, a man trudged along a road that led to the Chapel of Our Lady of Light in Santa Fe, New Mexico. The chapel was run by the Sisters of Loretto. As sun beat down on the man, he stopped to give water to his only companion, a donkey named Dusty.

He rubbed the donkey's soft ears. "Don't worry, we are almost there."

The man adjusted the pack slung over Dusty's back and gave a gentle pat to start their journey together. Soon they were on the streets of Santa Fe. Nestled in the midst of the town was the chapel of Loretto, next-door to a school for girls. The man tied Dusty to a tree and knocked on the door. He stood and waited, listening to women's voices talking energetically. It seemed to him they were saying something like *our prayers have been answered.*

A nun opened the door. She was dressed in long black robes and a black veil. Her face was flushed with excitement. Her name was Mother Magdalen.

She spoke in a confident manner. "Good morning. My name is Mother Magdalen. May I help you?"

He took off his cap and bowed politely. "I am here to help you."

"I see by your toolbox that you are a carpenter. Is that correct?"

He nodded agreeably.

"We have a big problem. An architect from France designed this beautiful chapel, small though it is, complete with a choir loft built high above the floor. Sadly, the architect died, leaving no plans for stairs to reach the loft. It is a tight space with no room for stairs," she raised her hands in despair. "We don't know what to do."

The man listened intently but said nothing.

"Can you help us?"

"I will build you stairs on one condition. I must be allowed to work in privacy. When I am working, no one is allowed in the chapel."

"Agreed!" Mother Magdalen said and shook hands with him, sealing the deal.

Mother Magdalen rushed back into the convent to share the good news. "Can you believe this? On the ninth day of our novena to St. Joseph, a carpenter appears at our door. God is so good!"

The other sisters listened with delight. "What is his name?"

"I don't know. He did not tell me."

Sister Rose, the youngest and most curious, asked. "What did he look like?"

"Well, he had a gray beard and gray hair…and a donkey."

"You mean like St. Joseph?" Sister Rose asked.

"Exactly," Mother Magdalen replied. She began to wonder if maybe, just maybe he *was*…." She shook her head and said to herself *now that's a silly thought.*

Over the course of several months, the nuns went about their business praying, doing chores, and teaching at the school. All the while, they heard sawing and hammering from dawn until dusk. Every day they brought a bowl of water for Dusty, who patiently stood under the tree. During this time, Sister Rose nearly burst with curiosity as she thought about the carpenter.

One day she left her room early, before the others were awake, and tiptoed to the chapel. Quietly, she opened the door and saw the man take a piece of wood, measure it, hold his saw and cut it with great precision. As he did, sunlight streamed through the stained-glass windows covering him in a halo of light. Sister Rose gasped and thought *maybe, just maybe he is the real…* Sister Rose returned to her room and told no one of her encounter.

Several weeks passed until one day the nuns noticed that silence reigned in the chapel.

"He must be finished," Mother Magdalen said.

All of the sisters crowded around Mother Magdalen as they opened the door. Before their eyes was a spiral staircase; its dark wood gleamed like starbursts. It made two complete turns from floor to loft and had no center pole for support. This made Mother Magdalen nervous. Would it be strong enough to carry the weight of a person?

"Would anyone like to volunteer to climb the stairs?"

Instantly, Sister Rose sprang into action, counting thirty-three steps all the way to the top. She spread her arms in triumph.

"Praise God," she said.

"Looks like the staircase works fine. Let's go find the carpenter and pay him," Mother Magdalen said.

Much to the dismay of Mother Magdalen, the bearded carpenter was nowhere to be found in the chapel. Dusty was not tied to the tree, nor was the man in sight.

"Mister carpenter! Hello! Where are you?" Mother Magdalen called.

No answer.

"Sister Rose, come with me. We will go door to door in the town, asking if anyone knows of the carpenter."

All day, they knocked on doors. Every time it was the same answer. No one had seen the man. In fact, no one knew anything about the man. By day's end, Mother Magdalen was perplexed. Not only could they not pay the man, they could not even thank him. An idea came to her.

"I will visit the lumber yard and ask them to look at the stairs. Perhaps they will recognize the wood and have a bill from the man."

The following morning Mr. Gomez, owner of the lumber yard, came to appraise the staircase. Upon entry into the chapel, he took off his cap and scratched his head in amazement. "I have never seen anything more beautiful!" he exclaimed and gently touched the smooth, shiny rails.

"Do you sell this kind of wood?" Mother Magdalen asked.

"We do not sell anything like this. In fact, this is some kind of spruce that does not grow in these parts. I can't help you, Mother. It will just have to be a mystery."

That evening Mother Magdalen led a litany of the saints. When they came to Saint Joseph, she looked up at the stairway that rose up to the choir loft. A smile crossed her face as she whispered a heartfelt thanks for the marvelous ways of God.

THE HOLY FACE OF JESUS
ITALY - 1898

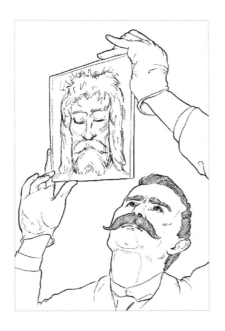

Silently, Secondo Pia crept through the darkened cathedral. Two men followed him, each carrying photographic equipment, including electric lights and a portable generator. Only one light shone. The red sanctuary light flickered near the tabernacle. Secondo genuflected and reverently moved toward a strange cloth, ancient in origin, displayed near the altar. He saw the ghostly image of a bearded man imprinted on a fourteen-foot piece of linen. Many believed it to be the burial cloth of Jesus. Now, for the first time, the Church had allowed a photographer to take pictures of the shroud. The year was 1898.

Secondo started his generator and turned on the light. He checked the equipment, carefully placing the camera on a tripod. It was a large camera with a wooden box and bellows behind the lens, covered by a black light-tight cloth. He lifted up the cover and placed a delicate glass plate inside the camera; the plate was coated with chemicals designed to capture an image. All was ready. He signaled to his assistants to turn on the generator and hold up the lights over the shroud. Secondo uncapped the lens and left it open to light for several seconds. That was the old-fashioned way to take a picture. Digital cameras would not be invented for another hundred years. Secondo took a deep breath and put back the lens cap. Quickly, they gathered up the equipment and headed to a dark room to develop the photograph.

By now it was midnight and time was of the essence. Secondo hoped that he had captured a visible image of the shroud. As they rushed through the streets of Turin, Secondo thought about the ancient relic he had just photographed. It was so mysterious that even a sharp-eyed observer could barely figure it out. Would observers understand the image? They hurried on into the night, turned a corner and burst into his studio, wasting no time. He set up his darkroom where the glass plate would be developed.

Secondo put on a work apron and gloves, poured chemicals into a developing tank, and submerged the plate into a solution. It would take some time for the image to emerge. Many doubts raced through his mind. After all, no one had ever used electric lights in a photography session. Thomas Edison had only invented the incandescent light bulb twenty years earlier. Secondo did not feel like a pioneer in photography. In fact, he felt like his experiment was on the verge of failure. All he could do was lean over the developing tank and wait.

And then it happened.

A face emerged from the photographic plate. It was the face of a bearded man with long hair and a swollen eye. It was the kind of injury sustained by a punch. With great care, Secondo spread another chemical over the plate to seal the image, thus preventing it from fading. Secondo picked up the glass plate and studied it carefully. It was the face of Jesus! How serene was that face, not that of a man filled with pain. Secondo remembered a bible verse from the Old Testament. *He was a man despised and rejected by mankind, a man of suffering, and familiar with pain.*

At that instant, Secondo felt his own heart break at the cruelty of man and the suffering of Jesus. Stunned by the revelation, he nearly dropped the plate. His heart pounded harder than ever before. *This is the face of Jesus!* Over and over, the thought raced through his mind. Secondo Pia had just taken an astounding photograph. By some unknown means, the faint image on the shroud was a negative. Take a photograph of a negative and you get a clear image of the subject.

If you saw a photograph of the real face of Jesus, what would you do? You would tell the world. That is what Secondo Pia did. After printing out the image, he carefully packed it and went to the publisher of a local newspaper who printed the story. A national newspaper picked up the story as did a Vatican newspaper. Wow! The face of Jesus was making the front page.

Sad to say, this fame brought trouble to Secondo. Some people said he was a fraud, that he had tampered with the print. Others accused him of making errors in his work. Secondo did not argue with them. He sighed and went about his work learning more and more about photography.

All this changed in 1931. A man named Giuseppe Enrie was given permission to photograph the shroud. Guess what? He looked into the developing tank and the face of Jesus stared back at him.

Several years later, an Italian nun named Sister Maria Pierina de Micheli created the Holy Face medal using Secondo's image. In 1958, Pope Pius XII declared a new feast day honoring the Holy Face of Jesus. It is called Shrove Tuesday and comes on the Tuesday before Ash Wednesday.

Secondo Pia did not live to witness this momentous event. If he had been alive, he certainly would have been amazed that the face recorded by his camera became one of the most famous photographs ever made.

MIRACLE OF THE SUN
FATIMA - 1917

Have you ever wondered what keeps the sun in the sky? That is a curious question to ask, you might say. Of course, God keeps the sun in the sky—most of the time. In fact, one day the sun did fall from the sky. It happened in Fatima, Portugal on October 13, 1917. Seventy thousand people witnessed this miracle, including three children who foretold the event.

Before the year 1917, Lucia, Jacinta, and Francisco were happy children who liked to play up in the mountains as they watched over flocks of sheep. Lucia Santos was ten years old. She was a responsible girl who kept an eye on her younger cousins, as well as the sheep grazing nearby. Francisco was nine and often wandered off in search of snakes to bring home to his mother. His sister Jacinta was seven years old and loved to twirl in the sunshine, dancing and singing joyful tunes.

One day all that changed. Little did these children know that God had chosen them to have heavenly visions that shook the world to its core.

On May thirteenth, all was quiet and peaceful. Oh, how lovely was that day with birds singing, bees buzzing, and daisies blowing in a gentle breeze. Suddenly, lightning streaked across the blue sky and then a second bolt flashed. Startled by the sudden storm, the children gathered their flock, eager to be in the safety of their homes. At that moment, a lady dressed in white stood on a small tree. Brilliant light, radiant like the sun, flowed out of her. Startled by the vision, they stood frozen in fear. Perhaps you would have run away from this vision, but Lucia and her cousins did not. Not only was the Lady beautiful, but she was kind and told them not to be afraid. The Lady spoke gently to them about important matters like heaven, hell, and the need to pray. Over the course of six months, the Lady appeared to them. As you can well imagine, it was impossible to keep these visits a secret. Many believed the children, but some did not. One day Lucia asked the Lady for a sign so that all would believe.

Here is what the Lady said, "On the thirteenth of October, I will send a sign."

This Lady always told the truth, for you see, this Lady was Mary, the Mother of God.

On the day that God arranged a miracle, you might guess that it would be a day filled with bright skies. Our God is full of surprises and this day was no different. On October 13, 1917, black clouds covered Fatima. Cold rain poured down on a crowd of seventy thousand people. Poor farmers, rich bankers, believers and unbelievers all stood in the mud; many huddled under umbrellas. Newspaper photographers snapped pictures of faces staring at the sky, not knowing what to expect.

Lucia and her cousins knelt in prayer by the little tree where the Lady again appeared to them. At noon, Lucia stood up and ordered the crowd to close their umbrellas. Storm clouds dispersed and the sun shone in a strange way. It appeared as a dull silver object, so dim that all gazed upon it without hurting their eyes. Suddenly it started to spin wildly, shooting off beams of colored light. Picture rainbow colors falling on faces and fields. It was like stepping into a wonderland.

After several minutes, the sun stopped spinning and the colored light disappeared. Now wait. The miracle had only begun. The sun began to revolve faster than wheels on a speeding car. Yellow light flamed out of the disc. Wonder turned to fear. To all who stood aghast at the phenomenon, it felt like the world was coming to an end. At this moment, the sun tore away from the sky and hurtled downward in a zig-zag path, fiery in appearance and intent upon total destruction. People screamed, terrified that the world was coming to an end. Many fell on their knees and prayed that God would forgive their sins. Judgment day had come. Jesus would descend from heaven and judge all peoples. That is what the frightened crowd saw, not all day, but for a short time. You see, the miracle of the sun lasted twelve minutes.

Suddenly at God's command, the sun stopped plunging to earth and returned to its place in the sky, shining like a golden ball. All was normal in the heavens, but not on the earth below. Stunned by the event, the people remained kneeling, shaking from head to toe, their clothes completely dry despite standing for hours in the torrential downpour. Newspapers around the world reported the event, complete with photographs of pilgrims staring in awe at the strange event in the sky.

So it was that Mary kept her promise. Many came to believe that Our Lady arrived to tell us that we must pray the rosary every day, especially pray for the conversion of sinners and to offer sacrifices to console the Immaculate Heart of Mary and the Sacred Heart of Jesus. To this day, millions of pilgrims visit Fatima to pray and to remember that day when God chose to shake the sun from the sky.

THE INCREDIBLE ESCAPE
FRANCE - 1940

Franz Werfel hid in a darkened room and listened to the crackling sound of an old radio. It was June 1940, and the Nazis had invaded France, conquering French forces in a short time. German soldiers hunted down Jews and killed them. Franz was Jewish and knew he was in grave danger. He leaned close to the radio and listened.

"Reliable sources tell us that famous Austrian writer Franz Werfel has been captured and executed by the Germans," the announcer said.

Franz felt like a noose was tightening around his neck. He and his wife Alma had fled Paris and settled in a tiny village called Lourdes. Located in a valley surrounded by the Pyrenees Mountains, it was the perfect place to hide out. As he looked at clouds blanketing Lourdes, Franz breathed a sigh of relief. German soldiers would never guess that he was hiding here. After all, nothing ever happened in Lourdes...or so he thought.

Not long after Franz and Alma arrived, they began to hear strange stories about a peasant girl named Bernadette Soubirous, a fourteen-year old child said to have had seventeen visions of the Blessed Virgin Mary in the year 1858. During those visions, a mysterious spring bubbled from the ground. It was discovered to have miraculous powers to heal. Soon thousands of pilgrims trekked to the isolated village. People who were blind, deaf, crippled, or dying came to bathe in the waters of Lourdes. Despite his desperate situation, Franz was intrigued. He wanted to learn all he could about Bernadette.

He talked to villagers and asked his wife to buy every book he could find on the subject. An idea percolated in his mind. Although a worldly man, Franz made a deal with God praying, "Dear God, if you help me escape to America, I will write a book telling the world about Bernadette and her heavenly visitor."

It is hard to imagine that a man running for his life would stop and talk to people about an event that happened almost one hundred years prior to his arrival. That is exactly what happened. In vivid detail, the people told of the day Bernadette was out collecting firewood for her family. She came to a river flowing with cold water, a stream she needed to cross. Bernadette hesitated. She was a sickly child, afflicted with asthma that made breathing difficult. Reluctantly, she sat on a rock, took off her wooden shoe, and pulled off her sock. At that moment, she heard the rustling of bushes near an oval-shaped hollow in a large rock. It was a windless day. What made the bush move? Was it a robber? Bernadette felt unseen forces were nearby.

Evil forces did not lurk in the brush. Quite the contrary. A beautiful young lady stood atop the bush. She was not a ghost, but a real person clothed in a shimmering white robe trimmed in blue. Golden roses rested on her bare feet and she had a gentle smile. Bernadette could not believe her eyes. Was it a dream? No, it was not. Overpowered by the sight, Bernadette fell to her knees and dug deeply into her pocket in search of her rosary beads. Still, she was too stunned to pray. The Lady also held a rosary made of shimmering ivory beads held together by tiny gold chains. In graceful motions, the Lady crossed herself. Bernadette imitated her and began to pray. The Lady moved her fingers along the beads but said nothing.

Franz listened carefully to the story, pondering its meaning. In some peculiar way, it touched his heart. Every day he visited the grotto, cupped his hands in the cool, clear water and drank deeply, all the while praying for a chance to escape from France. Time was running out. The Nazis were closing in on Lourdes.

Five weeks later, Franz and Alma made a break for it, aided by an American Quaker named Victor Fry. They met at the French town of Marseilles, where Fry arranged for them to cross the border by night, hidden in the bottom of a small sailboat. German soldiers discovered the boat and confiscated it. Next, they took a train to the Spanish border only to be thwarted by tight security. Hope was dwindling.

Franz closed his eyes and once again said his simple prayer. An answer came. Perhaps not the answer he wanted, but now he had no choice. Franz and Alma would have to climb steep mountains to escape. He looked at the towering peaks of the Pyrenees Mountains and thought about his bad heart and aging knees, but knew he had no choice.

Franz and Alma climbed trails filled with danger. German troops roamed the mountain paths looking for refugees. Partway through their trek, they heard voices. Border guards appeared and blocked their path. Franz thought for sure they would be captured and executed. For reasons he would never know, the guards did not arrest them. Instead, they directed them to a border crossing where security was loose. After paying the guards money that Alma had stashed in her clothes, the guards let them pass. Now they stood on Spanish soil, free at last.

Silently, Franz said a prayer of thanksgiving. Our Lady of Lourdes had answered his prayer. Now he had to keep his end of the bargain.

Franz and his wife arrived in New York in 1940 and then settled in California. In 1941, he began writing his book, *The Song of Bernadette.* Published in 1942, the story became a bestseller and was later made into a popular movie of the same title.

More than seven thousand recoveries have been attributed to the intercession of Our Lady of Lourdes and the miraculous waters. One of the most dramatic is the escape of Franz Werfel from certain death at the hands of German soldiers.

MIRACLE OF THE FLYING PRIEST
ITALY - 1943

In the year 1943 in San Giovanni Rotondo, Italy, a Franciscan priest named Padre Pio knelt alone in a chapel, deep in prayer. Like many Italians, he prayed for the end of World War II. It was a terrible war that had taken the lives of millions. British and American planes flew over the cities of Italy dropping bombs. As Padre Pio prayed, villagers entered the chapel. A man named Anthony was their leader. He quickly genuflected and walked briskly up to the priest.

"Padre, please help us. American bombers are flying nearer to us every day. We hear the drone of engines and the whistle of bombs dropping through the air and then bang...explosions everywhere. Rotondo is next. Oh, Padre, we don't want to die," Anthony cried.

Padre Pio tucked his hands into the sleeves of his brown robe. That was necessary, for he did not want anyone to see the blood-soaked cloths wrapped around his hands. You see, Padre Pio bore the wounds of Christ, miraculous marks called the stigmata.

The holy priest spoke calmly to Anthony, "Do not be afraid. Rotondo will not be bombed. God will see to that."

Now our story turns to a military airfield built on one of Italy's pastures. One man was in charge of the airfield. Bernardo Rossini was a general in the Italian air force. His assignment was to work with United States and British military. He was a serious man with great responsibility weighing him down.

Rossini muttered to himself. "I tell my pilots to bomb Rotondo and they can't do it. Either the bomber doors get stuck or the bombs are released and completely miss their targets. Always pilots tell some crazy story about a phantom flying near their planes."

The general shook his head in disgust. His thoughts were interrupted by a knock at the door. A young pilot entered the office and saluted.

Rossini spoke gruffly. "What is your report? Were you successful in bombing Rotondo?"

"No, sir."

The general slammed his fist on the desk. "You know that the Germans have an arsenal of weapons near Rotondo. It is vital that we destroy it."

"I know, sir. We tried but…" he hesitated.

"But what?" The general's voice rose in anger.

"When we pushed the button to release bombs, it jammed. We returned to our base and had it checked by mechanics. They found nothing wrong. I also saw…" Once again, he stopped speaking.

"What did you see?"

"I looked ahead and saw a friar in brown robes flying in front of us. He stretched out his hands to stop us. His hands were wrapped in blood-soaked cloths."

Abruptly, Rossini stood up and grabbed his hat. "Since no one else seems able to destroy Rotondo, I will do it myself."

With those words, the general arranged for a squadron of bombers to follow him, intent on destroying the German arsenal. As dawn broke over the airfield, Rossini climbed into the cockpit and revved up the engine of his airplane. He looked up at the sky, pleased by clear weather. It was a perfect day for dropping bombs. Four bombers followed as they taxied down the runway and rose high in the sky. The general gripped his controls and checked dials on the dashboard, careful to get the exact location of Rotondo. Certain he would put to rest the crazy stories of a phantom haunting the skies, he dipped slowly to the right and spotted a forest on the outskirts of the city.

Down below, he saw a brown object rising toward him. *It must be a bird, a large bird,* he thought. Closer and closer the object flew, until it was flying in front of the plane. Rossini stared in disbelief. A bearded friar held up his hands and waved at him, telling him to go away. His brown robe fluttered in the breeze, making him look like an enormous bird.

"It is only a mirage," Rossini said aloud. "Time to drop bombs."

Rossini looked down at his target.

"Now!" he yelled to the bombardier who pushed buttons that opened doors in the belly of the plane. Bombs spilled out and spiraled away from Rotondo, into nearby woods, exploding harmlessly.

Rossini stared down at the explosions and spit at the control panel, so angry was he. Not only was the general mad, he was also confused. He was a highly skilled pilot, able to locate targets with pinpoint accuracy. Still, he missed the mark. *I must be working too hard*, he thought. Rossini turned the plane away from Rotondo and flew back to the airfield.

You might think that is the end of our tale, one that sounds impossible but is verified by numerous eyewitnesses. Now here is the rest of the story.

After the war, General Rossini, who was a Protestant, visited the monastery located at Rotondo. He was eager to get answers to his many questions about the flying priest. Rossini knocked on the monastery door and was allowed to enter. Before him stood a group of friars. Among them was a bearded priest with hands wrapped in bloody cloths. Rossini introduced himself to the group.

Padre Pio came up to him, "So it is you, the one who wished to do away with all of us."

"Yes, Padre, I ordered bombs to be dropped on Rotondo, but every mission failed. Pilots always saw..." and then he dropped to his knees. "...they saw *you!*"

Contritely, Rossini bowed his head. "Forgive me, Padre."

Padre Pio gently touched Rossini's head and said a prayer. It was the start of a friendship that lasted for many years. One more miracle came from all these events. Under the inspiration

40

of Padre Pio, General Bernardo Rossini became Catholic, often telling stories of the amazing flying priest of San Giovanni Rotondo.

RESCUE OF THE
DIVINE MERCY IMAGE
LITHUANIA - 1948

In 1948, Communist soldiers busted through the door of St. Michael's Chapel in Vilnius, Lithuania, eager to steal or destroy sacred objects. Much to their dismay, the church had been stripped bare by Catholics who knew soldiers were coming and hid the objects away. Government officials also closed St. Michael's chapel to public worship. Only one work of art hung on the wall. It was an image of Jesus in a white robe with red and white rays streaming out of his heart.

The soldiers stared at the image.

"Should we tear this one from the wall?" one soldier asked.

"It is ugly. Let's shoot it up," the other said and aimed his rifle at the painting.

"Don't waste your bullets. Let's search for something more valuable," said the first.

Little did they know that this 'ugly' image was the original image of Divine Mercy painted by an artist under the direction of a Polish nun who had been instructed by Jesus to have the image created. In February 1931, Sister Faustina Kowalska was deep in prayer when Jesus spoke to her in a special way, so real it felt like He was standing there in the chapel.

"Paint an image according to the pattern you see, with the words, 'Jesus, I trust in you'," He said.

It was a confusing message because Sister Faustina was not an artist. Still, she trusted in Jesus. A wise priest named Father Michael Sopoćko believed in the visions as told by this humble nun and found an artist to paint the image. Under the direction of Sister Faustina, the artist created an image of Christ with his right hand raised in blessing and the left hand touching His heart. Rays, like blood and water, poured from his breast.

After the soldiers left the painting untouched, the image hung at St. Michael's Church until 1951. Lithuania was still controlled by the communist government of the Soviet Union and, thus, the painting was still in danger of destruction.

One day two women walked by the church. Bronė Miniotaitė and Janina Rodzevič noticed that the gate to St. Michael's Chapel was open. They entered the church. It was a sad moment for them. Here they saw the image of Jesus hanging in a cold, empty church. What if the little wooden church burned to the ground and the painting was destroyed? An idea glimmered in the mind of Bronė. They would pay off the guard and take the painting. That is what they did. Triumphant, they rolled up the canvas and walked briskly out the door, looking over their shoulders to be sure no one followed them. Bronė took it home and stuffed it in her attic. There it remained for many years. Here is the reason why.

First, you must know that the Catholic Church suffered greatly at this time. Why was this so? Leaders of the Soviet government did not believe in God and hated all that was holy. Priests, nuns, and people of good will were sent to prison for simply being Catholic. That is what happened to our heroine who rescued the painting. Bronė was sent to a work camp on the frigid tundra of Siberia, where she suffered for many years. During those dark times, she never forgot the painting stuffed in her attic.

Upon her release from prison, she told Father Józef Grasewicz, a priest who also had been sent to prison. He was a friend of Father Michael Sopoćko, who taught him about the Divine Mercy image. Father Józef knew it was important that the image be displayed to the public for veneration. Father Michael also believed that Vilnius was the true home of the Divine Mercy image. Vilnius was still under control of the Soviet Union. The painting was not safe in Vilnius. Once again, the sacred image of Jesus had to be moved.

As they unrolled the canvas, sadness filled their hearts. After years rolled up in the attic, the image was peeling and cracked, in great need of repair. Bronė had an artist friend who knew how to restore old paintings. She took the art to her friend, who did some repairs of the peeling image of Jesus.

Father Józef prayed that God would find a safe place to hang the painting in a church where it could be on public display. After many prayers, Father Józef smuggled the painting out of Lithuania to the Church of St. George in a country called

Belarus. At long last, the image hung high up on a wall over the main altar, a place where it could be venerated by the faithful.

In 1970, St. George's Church was closed by the Soviets. Once again, soldiers did not take the picture. They thought it would be too much trouble to get a tall ladder and remove it from a high place. The Divine Mercy image hung in an abandoned church for 16 years, alone but not forgotten. Who would rescue it this time?

Two nuns appeared on the scene, two nuns with a daring plan. Now was the time to return the painting to its rightful place in Vilnius. That was the request of Father Michael Sopoćko. They decided to find an artist who could paint a copy. The copy would then hang in place of the original. Sounds easy? Not so. We are talking about a painting that is seven feet long. That did not stop the two nuns. Our fearless heroines climbed up the ladder to a choir loft above the altar. Loose ceiling tiles made it easy to pry open a hole, pull up the original, and lower the copy into place. They cut the original from its frame, rolled it up, and spent the night at a friend's house. All night long, they prayed that they would escape and return the painting back to Vilnius, Lithuania.

The next morning the two nuns carried the long rolled-up painting on the platform of a train station. Police approached them, watching suspiciously. The nuns lowered their eyes and prayed harder. Each nun thought for sure that the police would seize the painting. The moment of truth had arrived. The police stared hard at them but kept walking, past the nervous nuns, leaving them free to complete their mission. With a tremendous sigh of relief, they boarded the train, their treasure safe, and they headed to Lithuania.

In 2003, the painting was restored to its original appearance and now hangs in the Sanctuary of Divine Mercy in Vilnius, Lithuania.

THE BOY WHO LOVED THE EUCHARIST
ITALY - 1991

CARLO ACUTIS

Sometimes we who live in the modern age think that miracles happened long ago, that saints lived in other centuries. Not true. As you will soon read, holiness is for all people in every age.

In the year 1991, a son was born to a young couple who settled into happy family life in Italy. They named their son

Carlo. His mother, Antonia, delighted in watching her son grow. In many ways he was like other children. Carlo liked to talk and eat and play with his friends. It was fun to make his friends laugh by drawing cartoons on the computer. Antonia noticed other qualities about her son. It seemed to her that God had given him special gifts, that he was very obedient to his parents and caring of other people. From an early age, Carlo loved to go to church and greet Our Lord in the Blessed Sacrament.

As Carlo grew older, an idea percolated in his mind. He knew about historic events involving consecrated hosts. Dozens of times in human history, consecrated hosts have turned to human flesh, and the consecrated wine turned to blood. The Church calls these Eucharistic miracles. Although some of these changed hosts are hundreds of years old, they still exist and are kept in churches for all to see. Carlo wanted to tell the world about these miracles. He asked his parents to bring him to these places where he would take photographs and post them on a website that he would design. As you might have guessed, his parents said yes.

One day his family planned a trip to Lanciano, on the hilly east coast of Italy. Here was the Church of Saint Francis of Assisi. Pilgrims from all over the world come to view a precious treasure. Lanciano is the location for one of the oldest and most famous of all Eucharistic miracles. It was important for Carlo to visit this site. He knew the story well.

Over twelve hundred years ago, a monk prepared for Holy Mass. Sorry to say, his heart was not in it. In fact, he did not believe that Jesus became fully present body, blood, soul, and divinity in the consecrated bread and wine. God had a surprise in store for him. At the moment of consecration, the host turned to flesh, and the wine turned into real blood. As you can imagine, the stunned priest began to weep.

Carlo thought of all these events as he entered the Church of Saint Francis. High above the tabernacle located at the main altar was a sparkling monstrance made of crystal and silver. Inside the monstrance was the miraculous host. Below the host was a chalice containing the precious blood. Pilgrims stood in line, waiting to climb stairs that led to the display. Carlo joined them, eager to see evidence of the miracle. Finally, it was his turn.

As he climbed to the top, Carlo felt excited. For all the world, it seemed like he was about to come face to face with Jesus. At the last step, he lifted his head and stared at the host that had changed to flesh. It was rosy in color and had no trace of white bread. In other words, it appeared to be an actual piece of flesh taken from a human body. Carlo peered at the consecrated wine. It bore no resemblance to wine. Five pellets of blood, irregular in shape, rested at the bottom of the chalice. Carlo had studied this miracle and knew what to expect. Still, he was shaken to the core. More determined than ever, he knew it was time to tell the world what he had seen.

Carlo continued his labor of love for Our Lord present in the Blessed Sacrament. Carlo and his parents traveled on the highways and byways of Europe, trips in which he photographed 136 Eucharistic miracles, all documented by the Church. He compiled them on a website, enabling him to send the world-wide message of Jesus alive in the Eucharist. Next, he designed an exhibit with large panels that displayed the photographs and told the history of each miracle. Thanks to Catholic organizations, this exhibition, called the Vatican Exhibition of Eucharistic Miracles, has appeared in parishes and schools throughout the globe.

As Carlo worked on this project, he noticed a change in his health. Once filled with energy and strength, Carlo began to feel weak and sickly. It became obvious that something was seriously wrong. It was time to visit the doctor. Tests revealed that cancer cells had begun to grow inside him. At the age of fifteen, Carlo was diagnosed with leukemia—a fatal form of cancer that forms in the bloodstream. On October 12, 2006, Carlo Acutis died.

Five years later, he was declared Servant of God, and his cause for beatification moved to the next phase. On February 21, 2020, the Vatican announced that Carlo had reached another step on the road to sainthood—that of Blessed. Imagine the reaction of Carlo's mother, Antonia, at this news. Of course, she was overjoyed, but she was not surprised. In the last week of Carlo's life, Antonia, had a dream.

"I had a dream of Saint Francis of Assisi who said, 'Your son Carlo will die very soon—but he will be considered very high in the Church.' I then saw Carlo in a very big church, high up, close to the ceiling, and I did not understand then."

After Carlo died, Antonia came to realize that her son's short life was part of God's plan, that Carlo was chosen to be an example to young people. This handsome teenager with curly brown hair and a friendly smile left behind many seeds of inspiration, including a quote that sums up his short life.

Jesus is my great friend and the Eucharist my highway to heaven.

WHAT SCIENCE
AND HISTORY TELL US

The Holy House of Mary

Of all the stories you have just read, the miraculous journey of Mary's House from Nazareth to Italy might be the most difficult to believe. That is a good attitude. In fact, that is the attitude of the Church with regard to miracles. Let us take a look at history and science to see if this story is worthy of belief.

First, we must ask a question. Why did angels carry the sacred House away from Nazareth? Eight hundred years ago, Christians were under attack by Saracens, who often destroyed churches. On May 18, 1291 Saracens captured a major city in Palestine, putting an end to Christian rule. To quote one historian, "eight days before that great catastrophe—for the consolation of the faithful and to preserve His former house from further desecration," God sent angels to move the Holy House out of danger. On the morning of May 10, 1291, the House was moved to Tersatto, Croatia, on the coast of the Adriatic Sea. Villagers awoke to discover a small building that seemed to appear out of thin air. It remained in Croatia for three years. Once again, the Holy House vanished. It reappeared in Italy.

Now let us take a closer look.

Here is the claim of those who believe in the angelic journey, an event known as the "translation" of Mary's House. From the period of 1291-1296, Mary's house was moved four times. The foundation is still in Nazareth, while the original structure is in Loreto, Italy. Scientific studies of the house look at construction material. After all, an old house built in Italy would likely be made of materials from the surrounding area. That is not the case.

In the late 1800's, Pope Pius IX requested a Church official to study the house and foundation. Cardinal Domenico Bartolini was an archeologist eager to help. Pope Pius IX gave him permission to take samples of stone and mortar from the foundation in Nazareth. Four samples were sent to Dr. Francesco Ratti, professor of chemistry at Sapienza University in Italy. Two samples were from materials taken from Nazareth and two were taken from the house in Loreto. Sources of the sample were kept secret.

Dr. Ratti discovered that the material was all of the same nature. What is that nature? Stone from the Holy House in Loreto is made of limestone, not red volcanic stone found in Italy. This limestone is identical to that found at the foundation left behind in Nazareth. Dr. Ratti also concluded that mortar holding the structures together was also a perfect match, further linking the foundation and house.

In 2014, Professor Giorgio Nicolini spoke at an international conference in Italy, sharing decades of research on the Holy House. One of his most important findings was that the dimensions of the Holy House in Loreto and the Nazareth foundation match perfectly, both in chemical composition and size.

Popes over the centuries encouraged veneration of the Loreto House. In 1624, Pope Urban VIII affirmed this practice, declaring December tenth as the Feast of the Translation of the Holy House of Mary.

Many saints have visited the Holy House of Loreto. Among those are Saint Francis of Assisi, Saint Francis Xavier, Saint Charles Borromeo (who made five pilgrimages), and Saint Theresa of Lisieux. In 1848, Saint John Henry Newman took a pilgrimage to Loreto and left with no doubt that there was a miraculous nature to the structure. "If you ask me why I believe, it is because *everyone* in Rome believes."

By the year 1917, forty-four popes had visited and expressed their belief in Mary's House. Among those popes were Leo XIII, Pius X, and Pius XII. In 1950, Pope Pius XII elevated the house to the status of a Holy Place. In 1993, Pope Saint John Paul II called the Holy House of Loreto the "foremost shrine of international import dedicated to the Blessed Virgin."

Generations of artists and architects designed a magnificent basilica that was built over the humble little House. Devotion spread far and wide. In 1920, Pope Benedict XV declared Our Lady of Loreto patroness of aviators. In 1927, Charles Lindberg carried a statue of Our Lady of Loreto on his historic flight from New York to Paris, becoming the first pilot to fly solo across the Atlantic Ocean.

The Shroud of Turin

When Secondo Pia photographed the Shroud of Turin, he stumbled into history. He could not have imagined that the image on this ancient linen was actually a photographic negative, revealing the face of a crucified man. His discovery sparked interest in the scientific community.

In 1978, over a period of five days, a team of thirty-three scientists worked around-the-clock, using seven tons of equipment to study every inch of the ancient linen. They concluded that the image on the shroud "is that of a real human form of a scourged, crucified man. It is not the product of an artist." Remarkably, these wounds match those described in Gospel accounts of Jesus' passion. The man in the shroud wore a crown of thorns, his face was beaten, and his side was pierced by a spear. Evidence also showed a man flogged over a hundred times.

Research proved that no medieval artist could have created such an image. If that is so, an important question remains. How was this sacred relic created?

Now we turn to Italian scientists, led by Paolo Di Lazzaro. Over the course of five years, they attempted to recreate the image. Using modern lasers, they aimed short bursts of ultraviolet light on a piece of linen. They failed to reproduce an image that matched the shroud.

Dr. Di Lazzaro concluded that the amount of ultraviolet light needed to duplicate the shroud image "exceeds the maximum power released by all ultraviolet light sources today." In other words, some incredibly powerful source of radiation burst onto a burial cloth over two thousand years ago.

For over forty years, scientists have studied the Shroud of Turin and come up with the same answer. They shrug their shoulders and say that it is a mystery.

Now we ask the ultimate question. Was the shroud image created by a spectacular burst of energy, like the explosion of a star, that occurred in the tomb where the body of Jesus was placed? Many religious scholars now believe that the Shroud of Turin is evidence of the actual Resurrection of Jesus Christ.

Image of Our Lady of Guadalupe

Like the Shroud of Turin, scientists have studied the cloak of Juan Diego using modern laser technology. Several findings have been published.

One fact that cannot be questioned is the age and condition of this rough piece of cloth worn by the humble peasant. It is over five hundred years old and still in good condition. Similar cloaks fall apart after fifteen years. For the first one hundred years, the tilma was not protected by glass. It was exposed to soot, candle wax, and human touch. This should have caused fibers to fall apart.

The original picture of the Blessed Mother was not painted by an artist. This conclusion was reached by Dr. Philip Serra Callahan, who photographed the relic under infrared light. He found no signs of a sketch, no brush strokes and no corrections. In fact, it appears to have been created in one step. As every artist will tell you, creation of a painting takes many steps from rough drawing to finished piece. Paintings simply do not appear magically out of a paintbrush in one motion. He also noted that the image itself has not cracked or peeled.

Richard Kuhn, who won the Nobel prize in biochemistry, also studied the cloak. His conclusion? He could not pin down the pigments to any natural source, either animal, vegetable, or mineral.

Technology has revealed a strange phenomenon concerning the eyes of Our Lady on the tilma. One engineer amplified the eyes twenty-five thousand times. Amazing reflections appeared. The microscope revealed images of the bishop and witnesses at the time Juan Diego opened his cloak. These reflected images follow the curve of the cornea. An artist who lived in the 1500's could not have such knowledge of eye structure.

Crowds of pilgrims come each year to the cathedral built on Tepeyac Hill in Mexico City. Church historians note that the appearance of Our Lady in Guadalupe was the source of millions of conversions, bringing messages of strength and hope. A change of heart is a wondrous miracle. As Jesus says in the Gospel of Luke: "In the same way, I tell there is joy before the angels of God over one sinner who repents."

On July 31, 2002, Juan Diego was canonized by Pope John Paul II. The feast day of Saint Juan Diego is December ninth.

The Eucharistic Miracle of Lanciano

The Boy Who Loved the Eucharist tells the story of Carlo's visit to the Church of Saint Francis located in Lanciano, Italy. Here two reliquaries are kept. One holds a piece of Flesh, a consecrated Host, that had once been under the sacramental veil of bread. The other holds five droplets of consecrated Blood, that had been under the sacramental veil of wine. Carlo was deeply moved by the experience. This miracle is the most famous of all Eucharistic miracles, dating back more than 1200 years. Two major scientific studies have been conducted on the Eucharistic miracle of Lanciano.

In 1970, the Church allowed the first modern study of the two extraordinary species. It was conducted by Dr. Edward Linoli, a professor of anatomy, histology, chemistry, and clinical microscopy. He concluded that the Flesh was heart tissue from a living human being. The Blood was human blood, type AB. That matches blood samples found on the Shroud of Turin and is a common blood type in Middle Eastern people. No traces of salt, preservatives or any other embalming chemicals were found. Both species should have deteriorated centuries ago.

In 1973, the World Health Organization conducted a study to verify Dr. Linoli's findings. This scientific study by a secular organization lasted fifteen months and included five hundred tests. Scientists backed up Dr. Linoli's studies. Once again, the Flesh was found to be living heart tissue, type AB blood, and no traces of embalming chemicals were found. In 1976, they released the study, declaring that they were unable to give any explanations for their finding. In other words, the Eucharistic Miracle of Lanciano is beyond the reach of science.

St. John Bosco

Many books have been written about Saint John Bosco (1815-1888). He is a saint known for starting schools for troubled youth, using gentle discipline, and instructing young people on the ways of holiness. He also wrote many books, including his autobiography *Memoirs of the Oratory of Saint Francis de Sales*. In the last chapter, Don Bosco wrote stories about Grigio's sudden appearance in times of danger, only to disappear when trouble passed. It is estimated that Grigio was seen from 1852-1883. Thirty-one years far exceeds the life span of any dog. During that time, many saw the wolf-like animal, including a group of religious sisters.

On several occasions, Bosco tried to find the origins of Grigio but was not successful. Over time he came to believe that Grigio was a gift from God. In his memoirs, he concluded, "What does it matter? What counts is that he was my friend. I only knew that the animal was truly providential for me on many occasions when I was in danger."

Miracle of the Sun

Many newspaper and personal accounts exist describing the miracle of the sun in Fatima, seen by an estimated crowd of seventy thousand pilgrims. Both witnesses quoted below are from reporters not connected to the Catholic Church.

One of the most detailed descriptions was written by Professor Jose Maria de Almeida Garrett, who observed the event in a calm, unemotional state of mind. He wrote, "suddenly one heard a cry of anguish breaking from all the people. The sun, whirling wildly, seemed all at once to loosen itself from the firmament and, blood red, advance threateningly upon the earth as if to crush us with a huge and fiery weight. The sensations during those moments were truly terrible."

Another description was published in a Portuguese newspaper by journalist Avelino De Almeida who came that day hoping to witness a hoax. Instead, he saw a solar phenomenon. "Before the astonished eyes of the crowd, whose aspect was biblical as they stood bareheaded, eagerly searching the sky, the sun trembled, made sudden incredible movements outside all cosmic laws—the sun 'danced' according to the typical expression of the people."

People from twenty miles away also saw the sun acting in a strange manner. Portuguese poet Antonio Lopez Viera wrote this account. "On that day of October 13, 1917, without remembering the predictions of the children, I was enchanted by a remarkable spectacle in the sky of a kind I had never seen before. I saw it from the veranda."

Father John De Marchi spent seven years in Fatima (1943-50) interviewing witnesses to the event. He wrote, "their ranks included believers and non-believers, pious old ladies and scoffing young men. Hundreds, from these mixed categories, have given formal testimony. Reports do vary; impressions are in minor details confused, but none to our knowledge has directly denied the visible prodigy of the sun."

In 1930, the Catholic Church affirmed that the miracle of the sun was an event supernatural in character.

Divine Mercy

On February 22, 1931, Sister Faustina Kowalska, a Polish nun, had a vision of Jesus dressed in a white robe, his right hand raised in blessing, with white and red rays pouring from his heart. Jesus asked her to paint an image "after the pattern that you see." With the help of her confessor Father Michael Sopoćko, they agreed to hire an artist named Eugeniusz Kazimirowski. He completed the painting in six months. Thus began a long journey in which the painting was hidden in an attic, hung in an empty church for 16 years, and exposed to the elements. It escaped destruction by hostile soldiers and poor attempts by artists to restore the peeling image.

Another chapter can be found in the history of Divine Mercy. This devotion was controversial in the history of the Catholic Church. On March 6, 1959, Pope John XXIII banned "images and writing that promote devotion to Divine Mercy."

Despite this condemnation, one Polish priest did not give up on Divine Mercy devotion. In 1965, Karol Wojtyla, the future Pope John Paul II, started an investigation. He discovered that condemnation by the Church had been based on poor French and Italian translations of Sister Faustina's diary, not on the original Polish written by Sister Faustina.

In April of 1978, the ban against the Divine Mercy devotion was lifted. Two decades later, Pope John Paul II canonized Sister Faustina Kowalska and declared the Sunday after Easter to be officially known on the Church calendar as Divine Mercy Sunday.

About the Author

Born in Boston, Kathryn Griffin Swegart earned a master's degree from Boston College. She and her husband raised three children on a small farm in Maine. Kathryn is a professed member of the Secular Franciscan Order and author of the best-seller *Heavenly Hosts: Eucharistic Miracles for Kids.* Learn more about her inspiring books for children at kathrynswegart.com

About the Illustrator

John Henry Folley studied Art at the University of Notre Dame and in a classical atelier in Manchester, NH. His illustration work rounds out a studio practice of oil painting to produce works on commission and for sale. He lives and paints in Massachusetts with his wife and children.

To see more of his art visit his website at www.johnfolley.com

Printed in Great Britain
by Amazon

29112228R00040